7-08

Since We're Friends

Celeste Shally

Illustrated by David Harrington

Awaken Specialty Press

To my husband Mike
We're in this together.

P.O. BOX 491 Centerton, Arkansas 72719
Or visit our website at www.awakenspecialtypress.com

ISBN-13:978-0-9794713-0-8
ISBN-10: 0-9794713-0-3

Library of Congress Control Number: 2007902104

Text Copyright © 2007 by Celeste Shally
Illustrations Copyright © by David Harrington

Printed in Hong Kong

Foreword

One in 150 children is diagnosed with an autism spectrum disorder. This means that just about everyone knows or will soon know someone who is autistic.

Many children with autism are able to take part in mainstream activities and attend a regular school, but they often need a little extra help along the way. With the proper support and understanding, children with autism can participate fully and meaningfully in their communities.

Most often we think of this support coming by way of a therapist, a classroom aide, or even a special technology. But in many cases it arrives in the form of a caring, considerate classmate or friend. Children are natural advocates, not in Washington, D.C., or their state legislatures, but in their everyday lives. They don't see differences the way adults do. They just see potential new friends. **Since We're Friends** describes how one child can make a huge difference in another's life, just by being himself. In this book, children learn that their actions matter, that their voices can be strong and loud, and that love, understanding, and compassion can profoundly change another's life—and improve our world in the process.

One voice at a time. One person at a time. Autism Speaks. Our children are listening.

Alison Singer
Executive Vice President, Autism Speaks™

It's finally summer vacation! It's going to be perfect because I'm going to hang out with my friend Matt who lives across the street. We have tons of fun together because we like the same things.

Matt acts a little different from my other friends though. He has autism. That means his brain works different from mine. He thinks about and feels things in a different way than I do. But we still have a great time together.

We both love sports. Football, basketball, baseball, soccer, you name it, we play it. We play on the Cougars basketball team together. Matt is good at scoring, and I'm good at dribbling and passing. We make a good team because we work together.

Sometimes Matt has a hard time following directions at practice. He doesn't always understand what the coach is saying. It's hard for him to listen when the gym is really loud.

Since we're friends, I show Matt what to do.

We have a lot of fun riding the swings at the park. We like to swing super high and pretend we're on a rocket ship blasting off into outer space! Sometimes our feet touch the clouds.

If someone is on Matt's favorite swing, he gets very upset and starts yelling. It makes him feel happy to play something the same way every time. Since we're friends, I try and think of something to do while we're waiting...like playing soccer or football.

Matt is very interested in animals. When Matt is interested in something, he wants to talk about it all the time! We look at books and watch movies together about animals.

We walk around the block together and make up crazy names for the neighborhood dogs. Then we feed them treats through the fence. Since we're friends, I don't mind talking about animals a lot because I like them too.

Matt and I go to the pool almost every day. We bring squirt guns, balls and other toys with us. We soak our football with water and try to splash each other with it. We slide down the water slide and then chase each other with squirt guns and attack!

Sometimes kids take our toys without asking. Matt gets frustrated and anxious. He is worried the kids are going to take the toys home and never give them back.

Since we're friends, I figure out a way we can all play together so Matt can stop worrying and be calm.

When the pool is closed for repairs, Matt gets furious. He doesn't like it when our plans suddenly change. I feel disappointed too.

Since we're friends, I think of a new plan and invite Matt to my house to run through the sprinkler. We spray each other with the hose and pretend we're firefighters.

At night, kids from our neighborhood get together to play freeze tag. Matt and I like to play because we can run as fast as lightning!

Some kids think Matt is weird because it's hard to understand the way he talks. They don't want him to play because sometimes he acts wild when he's excited.

Since we're friends, I don't want him to feel left out so I ask Matt if he wants to play tag with me and my friends.

Matt and I always have so much fun together. When it's time for one of us to go home, Matt gets stubborn and sad because he doesn't want the fun to stop.

Since we're friends, I make it easier for him and invite him to come over for breakfast in the morning. I give Matt a high five and say "I'll see you tomorrow!"